Pete and the Five-a-Side Vampires

by

Malachy Doyle

illustrated by Hannah Doyle

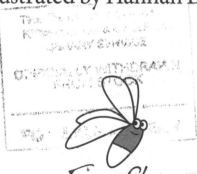

Firefl...

First published in 2014
by Firefly Press
25 Gabalfa Road, Llandaff North, Cardiff, CF14 2JJ
www.fireflypress.co.uk

Text © Malachy Doyle 2014
Illustrations © Hannah Doyle 2014

A CIP catalogue record of this book is available from the British Library.

Print ISBN: 978-1-910080-10-8
Epub ISBN: 978-1-910080-11-5

This book has been published with the support of the
Welsh Books Council.

Typeset by: Elaine Sharples

Cover design by Liz@madappledesigns.co.uk
Dragonfly series design by Laura Fern Baker

Printed and bound by: Bell and Bain, Glasgow

Contents

The Night of the Vampires

'Hey, Dad! Wake up!'

Pete ran into his father's room and started poking and prodding him.

'Oh come on, Dad! It's such a waste of time doing nothing for hours and hours in the middle of the long dark night. It's just so boring! Let's go out and have some fun!'

But his father only snored and ignored him.

So Pete wrote a note to say he was off to the park to get in some kicking practice. And he took Blob the basset hound instead.

Pete wasn't much of a sleeper, see. He just didn't get the idea of spending half your life in bed when you could be out and about, doing stuff. And the night was always so ... exciting. It was such a shame to waste it.

So he pulled out his very special night-time ball, the one with the light inside, and hoofed it down the lane.

Blob wagged and woofed and off he raced after the ball, with Pete chasing behind.

Kick, bark, run. Kick, bark, run. Down Westgate

 2

Street, over the Severn they went, and all the way to the park.

But there was a group of people there already, kicking a ball around, in the coal-black middle of the pitch-dark night.

And there was something weird about them. Weirder even than the fact that they were playing football in the dark.

And then Pete caught a glimpse of what was written on the backs of their ... cloaks. The Five-a-Side Vampires!

And do you think they played dirty, with a name like that? They certainly did!

Did they dive? They did. Did they push? They did. Did they trip each other up? You can bet your bottom dollar.

And what do you think was the worst thing they did when they got annoyed? Or when they got hungry? Or when they got thirsty?

They sunk their fangs into one another's necks!

Yuk! Double-decker yuk! Triple-decker gory gruesome eeky-beeky vampire yuk!

But was Pete scared? No way! He was a Night-time Wanderer, and Night-time Wanderers are brave as brave can be.

'They're the filthiest players I've ever seen, Blob!' he said, delighted. 'What they need is a ref, to keep them under control!'

And Blob said nothing, because bassets can't talk.

So Pete tucked the ball into his bag and pulled out his extra-loud whistle, the one he always carried with him when he went out looking for excitement in the long dark night. Handy, in case you get lost. Useful, in case you meet a bunch of blood-sucking vampires acting up on the football pitch.

'WHEEE, WHEEE, WHEEE!'

he went. 'Now get your act together, you lot! I don't care if you're alive or dead, ghosts or ghoulies. I'm the ref from now on, and we'll have a bit of fair play round here!'

Pete was proper Welsh, see – scared of nothing.

'We're not allowed to foul?' asked Vladimir Vampire, giving him the evil eye.

'That's right!' said Pete, facing up to him.

'No diving, pushing or tripping?' said one of the others.

'Not with me as ref,' said Pete.

Veronica Vamp sidled up close to him. 'No biting people when they annoy you?' she asked, breathing down his neck.

'Certainly not!' said Pete, stepping away sharpish. 'One go of that and you'll be off the pitch and back in your coffin before you can say Gareth Bale!'

Blob the basset growled at her, and Veronica slipped away.

'Well, that'll be no fun at all then!' snapped Gnasher, the other team's goalie, chucking the ball at Pete. 'I mean, what's the point of being a vampire if you can't nibble people's necks?'

'This is football, not breakfast!' Pete was staring him out. 'So while I'm the ref, you do as I say! Now PLAY!'

'Well, there's no way we're starting the game all over again just because some kid we've never seen before appears out of nowhere and starts bossing us about,' said Gnasher, baring his teeth. 'My side's one nil up already, right? You're not planning to take our goal away, are you?'

'Fair enough, you can keep your score,' said Pete, with a shrug of his shoulders.

Veronica Vamp waited for the kick-off and thumped it past Gnasher, way down the other end of the field.

'GOAL!' she yelled. But Pete didn't blow for it.

'GOAL! IT'S A GOAL!' screeched the furious vampire, dashing over to him, teeth bared.

But Blob, who'd been racing up and down the line, being a ball-dog, came haring onto the pitch – bark, bark! – to defend his bestest friend.

Veronica stepped back a bit as the brave young basset snapped and snarled at her pretty-pink vampire boots. 'OK, OK!' she said, dancing away from his snapping. 'Keep your fearsome fangs to yourself, mutt!'

Because maybe you didn't know, but vampires don't like dogs, see. Neither do ghosts, zombies or werewolves. That's why it's a good idea to bring one with you if you're out and about walking in the pitch-dark night. That and a whistle.

'And you can keep your fearsome fangs to yourself too, Veronica Vamp!' said Pete, eyeing up the sharpness of her red-stained teeth, coming dangerously close to the soft skin of his neck again. 'So what's your problem, anyway?' he asked her.

'IT WAS A GOAL, REF!' she screeched. 'The ball crossed the line, as clear as…' and her voice dropped as she looked all around, scared to say it, '… daylight!' she whispered.

Because that's the other thing vampires don't like. Daylight. They don't even like the word. It's bad for them, see. So bad that they have to be back in their coffins before the first rays of morning brighten the darkness, or else the poor unfortunate beings disappear, with a hiss, into nothingness.

But you probably knew that already.

'I didn't see any goal,' said Pete, shrugging his shoulders. 'It's too dark down that end of the pitch. So even though I'm sure you wouldn't be telling porkie-pies, I can't allow it, I'm afraid, Veronica. Refs can only call it as they see it. But I'll tell you what I'll do…' He whistled to Blob to fetch the ball the two of them had brought with them – the one with the light inside. 'We'll use this one instead. Then we'll all see it, no problem.'

The vampires gasped as Pete pulled the ball out of his bag.

'LIGHT!' they hissed, shielding their eyes.

'It's OK,' said Pete. 'It's just ball-light, not daylight.' Pete knew about the daylight thing. Most people do, these days.

So the vampires passed the ball around between them, and soon decided it was safe.

Pete was sorted now, too. He could see the glowing ball in the middle of the pitch-dark night, no bother.

But he did still have one little problem. One pretty big problem, as a matter of fact. And that was that Blob the basset hound was one hundred per cent convinced that the ball with the light inside was his and his alone. He just loved that ball, see.

So every time anyone kicked it Blob hared onto the pitch, grabbed it between his teeth, gave it a jolly good shake to make sure it had stopped breathing, and then carried it back to Pete. Waggity-wag.

And Pete had to restart the game. Over and over.

'Oh, will someone just BITE THAT DOG!' cried Vladimir Vampire, fed up because the other team had scored again, and were now two nil up. 'I mean, he doesn't know the first thing about five-a-side!'

'Yes, he does! He just likes getting his teeth into things, like you lot do…' said Pete, giving Vladimir a steely grin. Because you have to stick up for your best-ever pet, even when he is a bit annoying, now don't you?

And Blob sat at his feet and wagged. Waggity-wag.

'Well, I'll be the ball boy then, and Blob can play instead of me. Then we'll see what sort of a five-a-sider he is!'

So Gnasher launched the ball high (so Blob couldn't reach it) … Dracula's Daughter headed it on towards goal…

And who was there in defence, grabbing it and running, all the way back down the field and stabbing it straight past the goalie?

Who else but … BLOB! Who seemed to have got

the idea of five-a-side straight away (rather than just worry-the-ball-till-it's-dead, which is what he always did before).

The brilliant young basset, woofing for joy, ran past an angry Gnasher, grabbed the football between his teeth, gave it a good shake, just to prove it was really his, and then darted back to the centre spot. Waggity wag! Woof, woof!

'Well done, Blob,' whispered Pete, as quietly as he could so no one would think he was favouring one team over the other. I mean, you can't be seen to be doing that when you're the referee, now can you?

Then **'WHEEEE!'** he blew the whistle. 'TWO ONE!'

Dracula's Daughter ran from the pitch, screaming. She was a bad loser, see.

So Vladimir had to come back off the line and go on their team instead. (Because you can't have four in a team in a five-a-side game. Or that'd be eight.

Or is it nine?) Until he got crocked by Slurper Sue, who was going in for a tackle, hard.

Pete showed her a yellow card, but it was too late to help Vladimir.

'Aaiieee!' squealed the very sore vampire. 'That's not exactly lady-like!'

And he hobbled to the bench, clutching his poor ankle. 'That's me finished for the night,' he moaned.

So Pete gave him the whistle. 'Here, you be the ref, Vlad…' he said, 'since you're such an expert!'

So Pete came on and joined Bert, Slurper Sue, Ecky Edward and Blob, so they still had five a side. (Veronica had hobbled off with cramp by then.)

And the other side brought on Revolting Ronnie, to top up Verity V, Frankenstein's Folly, Horrible Harvey and Gnasher, in goal.

So it was five vampires on one side, versus three and a boy and a basset. So that's ten. Or is it nine?

And guess who got the upper hand? The team with the boy and the basset!

They kicked it and whacked it and thumped it, nodded it, shook it and stabbed it and…

'GOAL!' yelled Pete. 'TWO TWO!'

But then Bloodsucking Bert fell down in a faint.

'What's the matter?' said Pete, standing over him.

'He's run clean out of gas!' Vladimir told him. 'You stopped them sucking each other's necks, so they're all done in!'

Because that's the other thing about vampires. They don't eat, like we do. Or drink, like we do. No, all they do is suck blood. And if there's no blood to suck, they fall to the ground, exhausted.

'Tell you what,' said Vlad, from the bench. 'Now I'm the ref, it's back to vampire rules – you can be as bloodthirsty as you like everyone! Now get stuck in!'

Pete looked at Blob, and Blob looked up at Pete. And they both sat down on their bottoms on the cold wet night-time grass.

'What's up now, you pair of silly softies?' said Gnasher.

'We've had a bellyful of your bloodthirstiness,' said Pete, 'and now we're on strike for fair play, aren't we Blob? We don't really want our necks sucked, thank you very much.'

And Blob woofed in agreement.

'Well, we'll carry on without you then!' snarled Gnasher.

'We can't,' said Vladimir. 'It's five a side and there'd only be, eh…' He counted on his fingers. '… eight of us. Or seven without Bert…'

…who was eyeing up Pete's juicy neck with a mind to plunging his ferocious fangs in, as soon as he got the go-ahead.

So it was a bit of a stand-off. And things weren't looking too good on the human / dog front, as they were heavily outnumbered by vampires.

But suddenly there was a shout from the sidelines.

'PETE, *bach*! What in the name of nightmares are you doing out here in the middle of the pitch-dark night!'

It was Dad! In his pyjamas! He'd woken up and found his only son missing. But he'd soon guessed where Pete would be, especially with that footie-mad dog gone too. And especially when he'd found the note saying they were off down the park.

'We're playing five-a-side,' said Pete, 'with this lot.'

'But they're…' Dad stared at the fiendish faces, leering in at him, fangs bared. 'They're…'

'Yes, I know, Dad, but never mind. It's all good clean fun, isn't it, everyone?'

16

'As long as your team don't lose…' sneered Gnasher the goalie.

And everything went silent.

'What do you mean by that, Gnasher?' Pete looked all around, at each of the vampires in turn. 'What happens if we lose?'

The vampires laughed. In a nasty, vampire, sort of way.

'We suck your blood, kiddily-wink!' snarled Gnasher. 'We suck it till we're full to bursting!'

Pete looked at Dad, and Dad was blinking fast, like he was trying to work out if he was really awake or not. Trying to work out if he was in the middle of a nightmare, or in the middle of Llani football pitch, surrounded by real live VAMPIRES!

'I'd think of legging it, Dad,' whispered Pete, 'but even though they're a bit short of blood, I don't think they'd have much trouble catching us. Especially you. So we're just going to have to make sure we beat them in the game. Maybe you could join the team…'

'Me?' said Dad, gasping for breath. 'I haven't played a proper game of footie in ten years or more! Never mind against a bunch of...' he shook his head, afraid to even say the word '...who'd suck your blood as soon as look at you!'

'Come on, Dad – don't be such a scaredy-ba! We've got to win!' muttered Pete.

Blob was doing his best, but it was pretty much a two-man team by now (well, one boy and a long, low dog), because Pete's Dad was huffing and puffing and barely getting a look-in. And the two other vampires who were supposed to make up their numbers (Eeky Edward and Slurper Sue) were both stumbling about, weak at the knees from their lack of blood-sucking.

For some reason the other team didn't seem to have run out of energy in the same way. Pete suspected them of guzzling away at each other in the darkest corners of the park when no one was watching, but he couldn't prove it.

And by this time Pete and his team were three-two down and in danger of losing more than just the match.

'We've just got to win, Blob,' gasped Pete. 'Otherwise there'll be ructions, and no mistaking. They'll sink their teeth into us and we'll become vampires ourselves!'

Because that's who vampires are, see. They're humans who've had their necks sucked by vampires. (You knew that already, I suppose.)

Which is why it's a good idea to stay tucked up in bed all night, in case they're out and about and on the prowl. But try telling that to Pete and Blob.

(Mind you, they'd have to have been particularly bloodthirsty to try chewing Blob, considering he was a dog. But that wasn't going to help Pete much.)

'We're all done in,' said Eeky Edward and Slurper Sue. And they fell to the ground, exhausted.

'Uh oh,' said Pete. 'There's only eh…' He was looking around at what remained of his team. '*Un … dau … tri* of us left. We're in right trouble now!'

He booted the ball and up it flew, over the heads of the other team.

And guess who'd gone zooming down the field like a bat out of hell, and was lurking on Gnasher's goal-line, waiting for the ball to arrive?

BLOB THE BASSET HOUND!

He grabbed it with his front paws, did a quick one-two, and rolled it through Gnasher's legs. (Gnasher was all discombobulated, because vampires don't like dogs, remember?)

Luckily Vladimir the vampire ref didn't seem to know about the offside rule. Or because he was stuck on the bench, due to having been crocked by Slurper Sue, he couldn't see the angles properly.

Or hunger was getting the better of him, and he wasn't paying full attention.

'WHEE!' he blew, on Pete's whistle. 'THREE THREE!'

Knowing there wasn't a moment to spare, Blob grabbed the ball in his mouth, raced to the centre-spot and, without even bothering to shake it, he put it down at the feet of Verity V, the opposing team's main striker.

Straight from the kick-off, Pete stole it off her and booted it back down field.

21

And would you believe it? The ball with the light inside bounced once, skidded off a lump of mud and trickled past the wrong-footed, red-faced Gnasher.

FOUR THREE! They were winning!

Pete and his Dad were running out of steam, so Blob decided that the only way to hang onto their lead was to play the Vampires at their own game. To play dirty.

So what he did was wait in the darkest corners of the pitch, lying low to the ground in the shadows, wait for one of the opposing team to come running towards him and then run out in front of them. Trip!

It worked every time. The vampire went flying, Blob grabbed the ball, and they were back in possession.

Another twenty minutes of this and then…

'**WHEEEEEEE!**' went Vladimir Vampire, one last time. 'And the winners are – Pete, Blob the basset, Dad in his jim-jams, Slurper Sue and Eeky Edward!'

Everyone cheered, even though half of them had lost the game. Because the vampires weren't really all that bothered about winning or losing, now that they could get back to sucking each other's necks. Double-quick, so they'd have enough energy to scarper from the scene before daylight.

'See you again, Pete,' said Vladimir, licking his disgustingly red lips.

'Maybe you will, Vlad,' said Pete, taking the whistle from him, rubbing it on the grass to get rid of the blood and spittle, and then stuffing it in his pocket. 'But then again…' he said, winking at Blob and Dad, '…maybe you won't.'

Blob wagged, and grabbed his favourite ball.

And off they went, back through the last of the darkness. Back across the Severn, back up Westgate Street and home to bed.

'And next time you need to go out in the middle of the night, my boy,' said Dad. 'I'm coming too, right? It's not as if I want to – I'd much rather be catching up on my beauty sleep – but the sort of scrapes you get yourself into, Pete, you need someone sensible with you…'

Pete smiled at Blob and Blob smiled at Pete.

'Someone sensible like you, Dad?' he said.

And Blob said nothing. Because bassets can't talk.

The Night of the Werewolves

'It's too hot to sleep!'

It was the warmest night of the year, and Pete was tossing and turning in his bed.

So the next morning he rummaged about in the shed and found Dad's old tent – the one he'd used for going to festivals when Pete was little.

That night Pete was lying in his dad's old sleeping bag, in his dad's old tent. He was STILL all hot and sticky.

He threw back the cover, but it didn't seem to make any difference. Pete could hardly breathe.

 25

Listening to the sounds of the night, he heard the wind shushing up in Allt Goch woods behind him. He heard a car, somewhere in the distance… An owl, hooting…

He climbed out of the bag to throw back the front flap of the tent and let in some air.

And there, by the light of the rising moon, lay Blob, his ever-faithful hound. Good old Blob, keeping guard against the creatures of the night.

'Night, night, Blob,' he whispered.

The basset opened one of his big droopy eyes, and sort of winked.

Pete tried again. But it's never easy sleeping, when you're a Night-time Wanderer. Particularly when it's hot. Particularly when there's a big yellow moon, lighting up the night, making you think of all the exciting adventures you could be having, while the rest of the world's asleep.

Meanwhile the moon rose in the sky till, in all its glorious fullness, it was shining directly on Blob's face…

'HOWL!'

Pete nearly leapt out of his skin. It was the loudest, most blood-curdling noise he'd ever heard. Worse, even, that the heavy-metal records his dad dragged down from the attic every now and again and put on, full blast.

Worse, even, than Veronica Vampire screeching at him for disallowing her goal.

'Blob! Did you hear that horrible sound? What on earth was it?' gasped Pete, to the shape at the mouth of the tent.

Blob turned to him, and…

'HOWL!'

Pete's eyes nearly popped out of his head. Because there, instead of a normal-looking cuddly basset hound – all long and low and jowly – was a monster-dog three times Blob's size. With a head four times Blob's head, the longest ears in the history of doghood and great nasty fangs, fifty times their normal size, sticking out of its massive mouth.

It was still Blob, but he didn't look soppy any more. He looked SCARY!

'Blob!' gasped Pete. 'What's happened to you?'

But he knew what had happened, really. Because Pete was a bit of an expert on all things monster, and there was no two ways about it – Pete's cuddly basset hound had turned into some sort of a ... a weird sort of a ... doggy sort of a ... WEREWOLF!

'Oh crumbs!' he muttered. 'What'll we do now?'

And Blob, who deep down was still Pete's bestest-ever pet – despite having been transformed into a creature of the night by the light of a full moon shining on his face on the first Wednesday in August – crawled into the tent and licked him...

(Make sure you remember all that about the moon and the first Wednesday in August, my friend – it could come in handy one day. They tell you it's the full force of the sun you need to be avoiding these days, but the moon has powers we can only dream of.)

But licking his friend and master was the very worst thing Blob could have done, as Pete well knew (though he didn't have time to stop him). Because the touch of a werewolf's fangs on your skin … the dribble from a werewolf's kiss … the ucky-yucky smell as it slobbers its chops all over you…

Does one thing and one thing only (like when a vampire sinks its teeth into your neck). It turns YOU, the one who's being licked, kissed or slobbered on, into another … WEREWOLF!

'HOWL!' said Blob the werewolf.

'DOUBLE HOWL!' that was Pete, by the way – Pete the werewolf.

'Uh-oh,' he moaned. 'I've been and gone and done it now.'

And he tippy-toed back into the house to get a good look at the effect becoming a werewolf had

had on him. (And the reason he was tippy-toeing was because he didn't want to wake his dad and scare the poor man clean out of his wits. Not till Pete knew what he actually looked like, anyway. Not till he'd worked out how he was going to get himself back to normal.)

Up the stairs he padded, three at a time (being three times bigger than usual), and into the bathroom. Bashing his head as he went in, of course – being taller than the door. 'Duh!'

Then, 'Oh 'eck,' he said, looking at himself in the mirror.

Because yes, just like Blob, Pete's body was three times its usual size. His head was four times its usual size. His fangs, hanging down the side of his mouth, were fifty times the size of his dainty little teeth (and fifty times smellier).

And where he used to look sort of boy-in-the-street normal, he now looked distinctly MONSTROUS!

'At least I look like a *human* sort of a werewolf,' said Pete, looking over at Blob, who'd followed him up, 'and not a *basset-hound* sort.'

Because when you're transformed, in an instant, into a horrible-looking monster, you have to be thankful for small mercies.

I mean, Pete's teeth might be halfway down his chest, but at least his ears didn't dangle nearly to the ground, like Blob's did. At least he didn't look like a cross between a hippopotamus and the most enormous sausage in the world. (Pete was a bit surprised at this rather unkind thought, to tell you the truth. It wasn't the sort of thing he'd usually think about his favourite friend, Blob. But then, Pete was a werewolf now – and werewolves aren't best known for being all caring sharing cuddly.)

Pete got out his toothbrush and gave his choppers a good scrub. He took a swig of his dad's mouthwash, swirled it around and spat it in the sink.

Phew! At least his mouth didn't taste like the inside of a wellington boot any more.

And then a cheeky little smile lit up his face. Pete was always one for looking on the bright side of things.

'Hmmm,' he said to his doggy friend. 'I suppose, though it is a bit of a shock – being turned into a werewolf all of a sudden – that you and me could have some fun with this, Blob ... I mean, any excuse for a night-time ramble. And I'm sure Dad wouldn't mind – we're not likely to get into much bother now that we're werewolves!'

So off they went into town, to see what they could see.

Down Westgate Street. Turn right and over the Severn, with the moon glittering on the smooth-flowing water.

And down to the ducks, sleeping on the rocks in the middle of the river.

'**HOWL!**' went Blob.

'**DOUBLE HOWL!**' went Pete, giving it a jolly good go.

And the poor birds, frightened almost out of their feathers, took off with a fearful quacking. Under the bridge and away.

Then up Long Bridge Street to the Old Market Hall went the werewolves, where they sat on their hunkers and

'**Howl**ed!' yet again.

And the awful eerie sound echoed through the timber-frame of the ancient building, bounced around the arches…

Then up and down the town it went, and into the ears of its sleeping inhabitants (most of whom had their windows wide open because of the terrible heat).

'What's that?' said Mavis Davies, turning in her bed.

'Bit early in the year for Fancy Dress Night,' said old Will Thumbscratcher, turning over and going back to sleep.

'Nightmares again, is it?' moaned Hywel Hamer. 'Oh, this is BEYOND!'

Pete and Blob decided to move on, before anyone came out to see who was making all that fearful racket.

Quick as a flash – because another thing about becoming a werewolf is that it gives you super-human (and super-dog) speed – they zipped down Victoria Avenue to the donkey field, where...

'HOWL! DOUBLE HOWL!'

they went, one more time.

(Mind you, Blob wasn't quite as fast as Pete because, as you probably know, and if not you'll have seen from the pictures, bassets aren't exactly built for speed, what with their super-heavy bodies and their tiny little legs. Werewolf bassets have longer legs than normal ones, of course, but their bodies are MASSIVE, and oh-so-heavy, so they're still not the world's best runners.)

The poor old donkeys, shocked at the sight and the sound, galloped over to the far corner of the field, as far away from Pete and Blob as possible.

Pete looked round. 'You know what they say about werewolves?'

Blob shrugged his shoulders, in a doggy-sort-of way.

'They're indestructible,' said Pete.

Blob gave him a quizzical look. He wasn't very good with words of more than about six letters, never mind fourteen.

'It means you can't kill them,' Pete explained. 'You can't even hardly hurt them.'

So he raced round to the play park, hopped over the fence, climbed to the top of the slide and jumped off the platform into thin air.

'HOWL!' he went, as he fell (just for the fun of it). But somehow, without even trying, he twisted and turned, landed on his feet and didn't feel a thing.

So Blob lumbered up the slide and did the same. Which took a lot of courage, as well as a lot of effort, as bassets are not exactly well known for their jumping. Too much weight for too little legs, see.

But it worked, just like it did with Pete. Except he landed on all four feet, rather than two.

So then Pete climbed onto the swings, swung himself as high as he could, and let go.

'**Wheeeee!**' he yelled, flying through the air and landing on his feet yet again.

(Don't try this at home, folks – it is NOT a good idea. Unless you're a werewolf, of course. But if you are, what are you doing reading this? You ought to be out and about, scaring people!)

'Let's have a go at something higher! Much higher!' said Pete.

So they loped back up through town to the old bridge, leapt off, landed on the rocks far below, and didn't feel a thing.

(Guess what? Unless you're a werewolf, this is not the best plan, either.)

But as they were climbing back up the bank they saw a flash of torches.

'I thought I saw something,' said a voice. 'But when I looked again, there it was, gone!'

'Look – over by here!' said another. 'Who belongs to this footprint?'

'No, down by here!' said a third. 'I'm sure I heard a splash!'

And there, on the bridge, was a police car, lights flashing.

'Someone must have reported us, Blob!' hissed

39

Pete. 'Well, I suppose we were making rather a lot of noise.'

Pete grabbed a mighty tree and bent it right over so they were hidden in the thickest part of the leaves. (Because I'm not sure if I told you yet, but being a werewolf gives you super-human strength, as well as speed.)

The coppers made their way down the bank, slipping and sliding in the shadows and, just as they got close, Pete let go of the tree which shot back to standing position, sending one hundred and forty-six sleeping birds flying into the air. Squawk! Squawk!

The startled policemen looked up, just as…

'HOWL!' went Blob and Pete, in their very best werewolf howls.

And the terrified coppers fell into the river. Splash!

Pete and Blob ran up onto the bridge and crouched down behind the wall, watching to check the policemen got out of the water safely.

They may have become werewolves, and they didn't mind giving people (and birds, and donkeys…) a bit of a scare, just for the fun of it, but they didn't actually want to hurt anyone, oh no, because deep down they were still Pete and Blob. Yes, deep down, they wouldn't hurt two flies.

Then when they saw the trio of dripping policemen making their way back up to the squad car, they headed for home, double quick.

Except Pete had an idea.

'Let's nip in here,' he said, heading down Church Street.

So they leapt over the big high metal gate of the cemetery, and had pots of fun zooming up and down between the gravestones, jumping out on one another and…

'**HOWL**ing!'

They were having a barrel of fun, though I'm not sure what all the ghosts and ghoulies thought of it – they like to be left in peace, I'd say. And if anyone's scaring people in graveyards, I suspect it's supposed to be them.

'It's a good laugh being a werewolf,' said Pete, sitting on his garden wall, at last. 'But it's a bit weird, too, don't you think, basset *bach*?'

Blob just shrugged.

'I mean,' said Pete, 'I wouldn't want to be one for the rest of my life. In fact, I think one night's just about enough, wouldn't you say?'

Blob wagged his tail.

'So if werewolves are indestructible,' Pete asked himself, 'how do you stop being one, I wonder?'

Blob frowned at him. Too big a word again. Too long since he'd had it explained. (Bassets are dogs of little brain, I'm afraid. Big ears, but little brain.)

'We can't be killed,' Pete explained. 'Remember?'

And he went in and looked it up on Wiki-werewolf.

Stick a knife in its head, was the first suggestion he came to. 'No fear!' said Pete.

Hammer nails through its hands, was the next. 'I don't fancy that either – do you, Blob?'

Blob shivered his ears.

 44

Pete scanned down the page. 'Silver!' he said, at last. 'You have to be stabbed by silver, it says. Hmmm.'

The trouble was, Pete didn't really want to be stabbed. Not in his head, not in his hands, not anywhere, to tell you the truth. Not even gently, into his extra-thick werewolf skin.

Because even if you know it's not going to kill you because you're indestructible, it can't be very nice, sticking a knife in yourself. Or into your bestest-ever friend. Or having them do it to you.

And just because it was made of silver or gold or whatever – the thing you were being stabbed with – it wasn't going to make it any nicer. No way.

And anyway, just because it said on there that being stabbed by silver might stop you being a werewolf, what guarantee did you have that you'd go back to being normal common-or-garden boys and dogs?

'I mean, for all we know, we might become vampires instead,' said Pete, remembering their night in the park.

'Or zombies,' said Blob. Or he would have, if he could have. And if he'd any idea what zombies were.

'Or we might just disappear into thin air and never be seen again,' said Pete. Which didn't sound much like fun. 'Because if you destroy something, it's gone, isn't it? I mean, it doesn't just turn back into what it was before.'

And where were they going to find any silver, anyway? It wasn't something there was a whole heap of lying around in 14 Swansea Terrace. Any of, so far as Pete knew.

So they went back outside, curled up in the tent (well, one in the tent and the other in the doorway), and fell asleep at last.

Because it's a bit tiring, being werewolves … jumping off slides, swings and bridges … frightening ducks and donkeys, and giving the whole town nightmares… Being chased by the police, using trees as catapults, and scaring all the ghosts and ghoulies in the graveyard – that's all a bit tiring too.

Even if you've got super-human (or super-dog) speed and strength.

They woke up, to hear Dad calling.

'Pete! Pete! Are you all right in there? Pete – it's past ten o'clock! The sun's high in the sky!'

And, while his dad was speaking, Pete felt something strange happening. Like the reverse of what he'd felt when Blob had licked him, only a few hours before. Yes, his body was shrinking! His teeth were slipping back into his mouth! Whoopy-doo!

And he remembered having seen, when he was looking it up on the computer, that some people believed that there was one other way to stop someone being a werewolf (apart from stabbing them with silver, or through their hands or head, that is). And that was for them to say the person's name, three times over, just like his dad had done.

It seemed way too easy, though, when Pete had read it, compared to being stabbed and stuff, so Pete hadn't believed a word of it.

But it had worked! Dad had said 'Pete! Pete! Pete!' and it had really truly worked! He'd gone back to his normal size!

So Pete turned to his faithful basset, to see if it would work for him, too.

'Blob, Blob, Blob...' he whispered, before his dad got to them.

And his bestest-ever friend, thinking Pete was calling him, pushed his way into the tent.

Well, there wasn't much room in there for a boy and a werewolf three times the length of a normal basset, but luckily Blob's monsterosity slipped off him just as he came through the flap.

He was back to being a basset at last! A proper cuddly, droopy-eared basset!

Blob licked Pete, as Dad's face filled the doorway.

'Did you have a good night, you two?'

Pete nodded. 'Yeah, great,' he said.

'Not too warm for you?'

'I kept the flap open,' said Pete.

'No madcap adventures out and about on your own without a sensible adult?' said Dad.

Well, Pete just smiled. And Blob just wagged his tail.

The Night of the Bwca

It was Friday night. Pete was tossing and turning, trying to get to sleep, when he heard a knock, knock, knocking from somewhere in the distance. He got up and went to the window. It sounded like it was coming from the shed at the bottom of the garden.

Sometimes his dad messed about with things out there – fixing punctures, trying to get old radios to work, that sort of thing – but never in the middle of the night.

So Pete, glad of an excuse to be up and about, especially on a bright moonlit night, threw on his

night-time wanderer gear, grabbed his super-dooper beam-blaster torch and tippy-toed down the stairs.

'Yes, you can come too,' he whispered to his favourite-ever basset. Because there was Blob, beating his tail on the mat, waggity-wag.

'Knockity, knock,' went the noise, getting ever louder as they headed down the garden. 'Knock, knockity, knock.'

As Pete shone his beam-blaster through the window of the shed, there was a little squeal, the knocking stopped, and something slid out of view.

Pete ran inside, flashing his light into every nook and cranny. But whoever or whatever it was, they'd somehow disappeared.

And then he gasped – for there, on his dad's workbench, was a tiny little miner's lamp! Next to it there was a tiny little hammer. And next to that, there was a funny old clock, tick tocking.

'Weird,' said Pete, picking each one up and putting them down again. 'Super weird.'

Pete put the gas out in the lamp, in case it set the shed on fire. Then he left the lamp and the hammer on the table (they just might have been his dad's, he thought – though he was sure he'd never seen them before), and brought the clock back into the house.

It was an old-fashioned alarm clock, the type with metal dongers on the top. The really loud type.

In the kitchen, he set the alarm for seven o'clock, tiptoed into his dad's room and put it by his bed. Just for a laugh.

Then he went back to his room and fell asleep.

'RINGITY RING, RINGITY RING!'

It was morning, and the super-loud alarm was crashing through the silence.

'RINGITY RINNNGGGGGGG!'

'Aarrggh!' yelled Pete's dad. 'What's all that racket? Where's the fire?'

And then he saw where it was coming from. Pete heard him fumbling to turn it off.

'How did that old thing get here?' he was grumbling. 'And how come it's working? I've had it in my shed, meaning to mend it, for YEARS!'

But Pete didn't say a word about it, then or later. And neither did Blob.

The next night, lying in bed, Pete heard the little tap tap tapping noise again. 'Knockity, knock. Knock, knock.'

He grabbed his night-time gear, fetched his ever-faithful basset, and they tippy-toed down to the shed.

But this time Pete had the good sense to leave his torch behind. Whoever it was and whatever they were up to, he wanted to catch them in the act.

'Knockity, knock. Knock, knock,' he heard.

Pete threw the door open…

But he was too late again, for just as he did so,

something (or someone) squealed, slipped to the floor and disappeared.

Pete picked up the little lamp from the workbench (it was lit again) and had a really good look round.

There was no sign of anyone, but on closer inspection he noticed that one of the wooden floorboards was slightly wobbly.

Pete gave it a bit of a tug and the board shifted slightly. He held the lamp to the gap and saw a hole, going deep down into the ground.

Blob went over to it, had a good sniff and whined.

'Is there someone down there, do you think?' said Pete. 'Is that where the knockity-knocker went?'

Blob beat his tail on the floor. Waggity-wag. Woof woof.

'Weird,' said Pete. 'Very weird.'

So the NEXT night, which was Sunday night, he and Blob hid inside the shed.

First Pete went to his own bed, so his dad wouldn't get suspicious, but as soon as his dad went into his room, Pete slipped outside, taking Blob with him.

They were in there for ages, getting more and more uncomfortable, and more and more cold, and Pete was just about to give up and go back to bed – because it was school in the morning and he knew he'd better get to sleep, especially after the last two unsettled nights, or he'd find himself dozing in class and then he'd be in real trouble, when…

'A light!' whispered Pete. He'd slid the loose floorboard slightly open when they'd gone into the shed, and then kept his eyes fixed on the gap the whole time they'd been in there.

The tiny light, coming from the hole, got brighter and brighter, until someone or something slid it and the next couple of boards across, and out popped…

A little man! No more than two feet tall. With a dirty-looking face, a big hairy beard, pointy ears, and another little miner's lamp in his hands.

'Blimey!' muttered Pete, under his breath.

But he and Blob were as silent as mice, as up the little guy clambered, through the gap in the floorboards. Knockity, knock, tapping them back into place once he was through. Then up, onto a chair. Up again, onto the workbench … where he picked up his little hammer, and…

'Knockity, knock.' He set to work. Doing whatever it was he was doing.

'Hello there, little fellow!' whispered Pete, and the hairy little man nearly jumped right out of his skin.

'Who's that?' he peeped, in the squeakiest voice.

'It's me,' said Pete, from in behind the bicycles. 'Over here, in the corner, with my long, low dog.'

And the tiny fellow knew it was too late to run.

'But who are YOU?' asked Pete, when he and Blob had come out of hiding.

'I'm a bwca,' said the little man, eyeing them both suspiciously. Especially Blob.

'A booka?' said Pete. 'Like a book, with an "a" on the end?'

'No, a Welsh sort of a bwca,' said the man. 'With a "w" and a "c".'

'Oh, a BWCA!' said Pete. And then he frowned. 'What's that, when it's at home?'

'It's me,' said the tiny man. 'Me and my people. We're little miners, and we're called bwca because it's a bit like the sound of all the knocking we do.'

'Knocka, knocka – bwca, bwca?' said Pete.

'That's it,' said the man, bashing a bit of metal with his tiny hammer.

'So you're little miners?' said Pete.

'Yes,' he said. 'There's bwcas all over Wales – well, all *under* Wales, I suppose,' he said, with a giggle. 'But my lot have been here, in the Llani area, since the days of the lead mines.'

'Fair play. So have you always lived underground?' Pete asked him.

'Ah no,' said the little fellow. 'We used to share Up Top with your crowd, back in the olden days. But it's a bit dodgy now for little fellows like us, what with all those horrible speedy car-things. And big dogs…' he said, giving Blob a dirty look.

But Blob just smiled. Waggity-wag.

'So what are you doing here, in Dad's shed?' Pete asked him.

'Oh, we come up to the surface in the night, when it's quiet, sometimes. And, if we're feeling particularly helpful, we might do a few good deeds. But only for good people,' said the little bwca man.

'Like mending alarm clocks for my dad?'

'Yes, like mending alarm clocks.'

'And do you only do good deeds?' asked Pete.

'Oh no,' said the bwca, with a sly little smile. 'When there's a full moon, we're allowed to get up to all sorts of mischief!'

'Like what?' said Pete, who was partial to a bit of night-time mischief himself, as you very well know.

'Would you like to see?' asked the little bwca man.

'Yes, please.'

'OK. Come back tomorrow night. It'll be full moon then. Maybe you and me can have a bit of fun.'

Blob tapped his tail on the floorboards. 'And you, hound,' said the bwca, giving him a little sideways look. 'If you promise to be good.'

So the next night, Pete sat up in bed, reading. He was waiting for the telltale sound of the little bwca man.

Next thing he was fast asleep. He'd had too many late nights in a row.

But soon after that, there was a scratching at his door. And a whining.

'What's up, Blob?' he muttered.

And then Pete heard it. 'Knockity, knock,' from down the garden.

'Clever Blob,' whispered Pete. 'Let's go and find our little friend.'

'Hello, Mr Bwca,' he said, easing open the door of the shed. 'Howya keeping?'

'*Shw mae*, Pete. *Shw mae*, Blob,' said the miniature man, tapping away by the light of his lamp.

'But I thought you were going to be doing naughty things tonight,' said Pete. 'It's a full moon, remember?'

'Oh, I am,' said the Bwca, with a cheeky smile. 'I've just been waiting for you two. Let's go.'

'Where are we off to?' asked Pete, setting off down the road.

The little man shrugged his shoulders. 'I don't know,' he said. 'You're the one who has to decide.'

'What do you mean?' asked Pete.

'Well, remember I said we bwcas do good deeds for good people?' he said.

'Like my dad and the alarm clock?' said Pete.

'Exactly. Well, we do naughty things, too, like I told you, but only to nasty people. So who do you know that's nasty?'

Pete looked at Blob and Blob looked at Pete.

'Come on...' said the bwca. 'There's got to be at least one, even in a friendly little town like Llani.'

'Hmmm,' said Pete. 'Well, there's Billy Beggs...'

And Blob growled at the very name.

'Who's Billy Beggs,' asked the bwca.

'He's the school bully,' Pete told him.

'Perfect,' said the tiny man, with a sly little grin.

'But I don't want to actually hurt him,' said Pete, frowning. 'I mean HE's the bully, not me...'

'Oh, don't you worry,' said the little bwca-man. 'We'll just give him something to think about.'

And off they went, down Westgate, up Eastgate, and all the way to Billy Beggs' house.

When they got to the bully's back gate, the bwca got his miniature hammer out.

'Knockity knock,' he went on the lock, and it fell to the ground with a clatter.

'Shhh!' said Pete, as they tippy-toed into Billy Beggs' yard. 'If he sees us, we're done for! Or I am, anyway!'

But then…

'My bike!' gasped Pete, seeing it slap-bang in front of him, leaning against the wall. 'He's only gone and nicked my lovely bike!'

And Pete hadn't even noticed it was missing from his shed. But it had to be. Because no one else had one like it. It was the only Chopper in town.

Pete grabbed it – it was his pride and joy – but it was fixed to a drainpipe with a super-strong lock.

'Have no fear,' whispered his newest little friend. 'There's a bwca here.'

And pulling out his hammer, he tappity-tapped, and the lock clattered to the floor.

'YOU'RE A BIG BULLY, BILLY BEGGS!' yelled Pete, at the top of his voice.

And off they ran (and cycled), top speed.

'Who's next?' asked the bwca, back in Pete's dad's shed.

'What, you want another nasty person?' said Pete. 'Well … um … there's always Mrs Walters, round the corner… She's not exactly nasty, but…'

And Blob gave a happy little whine, at the thought of his arch-enemy getting her come-uppance.

'What's so bad about her?' said the bwca.

'Oh, she's just chopsy, isn't she, Blob? Always complaining about you yapping, though you only ever do it when you're happy…'

'Woof, woof,' said Blob, with a little doggy smile.

'And the worst thing is, she never gives us our balls back,' said Pete.

'Fair play,' said the bwca. 'Let's go and give her a little visit.'

'Tappity tap,' went the hammer, on the lock of Mrs Walters' shed.

Then, once he'd got it open, the bwca shone his lamp around. And there, in a giant net in the corner of the shed, was an enormous pile of balls.

'Wow!' said Pete. 'I knew she'd had a lot, but I never thought there'd be this many!'

And he started passing them out, one by one, counting them as he went…

'Thirteen, fourteen … fifteen footballs!'

And not only that – there were eight rugby balls, six Blob balls, four tennis balls, two cricket balls and a frisbee!

And Blob, who LOVED balls, and HATED anyone who stole them from him, had to grab every single one and give it a good shake. He was in basset heaven!

(Mrs Walters' house backed onto Pete's by the way, which is why so much stuff ended up in her garden. So all they had to do was kick, throw or frisbee them all back over. Easy enough, even in the dark.)

'That's that done, then!' said Pete, when they'd finished. But then he heard a 'Knock, knock, tinkle,' from behind him.

'That'll stop you telling tales, you silly grinner!' said the bwca. And Pete turned round, to see him bashing Mrs Walters' garden gnome.

'Oh, I do love bringing a bit of badness on someone...' muttered the bwca, with a happy little giggle. 'As long as they deserve it, of course!'

'OK,' said Pete, when they were back once more in the safety of the shed. 'I think that's quite enough badness for one night.'

'You're right,' said the bwca. 'I'm off back down to my little underground home. I'll see you two again sometime, maybe. And don't forget...' he said, just before he slipped down between the floorboards, taking with him his lamps and his hammers and any sign that he'd been there. 'We may be small, us bwcas, but we know how to look after ourselves. So if you ever hear anyone laughing at us, let me know!'

'What would you do?' asked Pete.

'I'd wait till it was dark,' said the little bwca man. 'And then I'd be up there to tap nails through the soles of their shoes, so that when they put them on in the morning, they'd stab holes in every single one of their little tootsies!'

'Oh,' said Pete.

'And if they were doing nasties to other people as well as mocking us bwcas, I'd lead them up a narrow path to the edge of a cliff in the middle of the night, then blow out the lamp and leave them there...'

'Well, we'd never say a bad word against you, would we, Blob?' said Pete. 'We won't let anyone else do it, either.'

And Blob said nothing, because bassets can't talk.

But he beat his tail on the floorboards, to show how much he agreed. Waggity-wag. Woof woof.

'And if they were extra-specially nasty, as well as trying to make fun of us,' said the little bwca man, 'then I'd grab them by the nose and banish them and their family to the banks of the Red Sea for fourteen generations!'

'Wow!' said Pete. 'You don't mess with the bwca!'

'Quite right,' said the little miner. 'Because when you're good, we're very very good in return. But when you're bad...' he said, his eyes darting from Pete to Blob and back again, 'we're HORRID!'

And with that and a giggle, he was gone.

'Phew!' said Pete. 'Is it just me, Blob, or is that little fellow a bit scary? I mean, it just goes to show, you don't have to be big to be bad!'

And Blob? Well, Blob agreed.

The Night of the Hell Hounds

'Aw-rooooo!'

Blob woke. What was that noise? It was coming from somewhere outside.

'Aw-rooooo!'

There it was again. He perked up his ears. Then he plodded over to the cat flap, where he could hear better.

'Aw-rooooooo!'

The hair stood up on the back of Blob's back. He pushed his head through the flap and stared out into the darkness.

And saw two hundred eyes, glittering back at him!

'Aw-rooooooo!'

Horrid-looking doggy eyes! Scary-sounding hounds! And whoever it was, they were calling him! Calling him to join them!

Blob tugged his head back inside, double quick. There's no way he was joining up with a gang of green-eyed night hounds. He was in a team already. Him and Pete. And he didn't like the look of that lot. Not one little bit.

He turned his back on the cat flap, clattered down the hall, up the stairs, and scratchity-scratched on Pete's door.

'What's the matter, pup?' Pete had been fast asleep for once, happily dreaming of monsters.

But at the sound of a distressed Blob, he hopped out of bed and ran to open the door.

Blob raced across the room, clambered up onto the bed, tugged the duvet over his head, and lay there, shaking.

'What's up?' said Pete, pulling back the cover and staring at the long, low shivery dog. 'It's not like you to be such a scaredy-basset! Have you been dreaming the same dream as me, by any chance? Nightmares – I love them!'

But then Pete heard it.

'Aw-rooooooo!'

And it wasn't just any old nightmare. It was real – and it was right outside his window. Which was even better, according to Pete.

He ran over to the curtain, pulled it back and…

'Aw-roooooo!'

He saw a hundred pairs of glittering eyes, staring up at him. And heard a hundred hounds, howling.

'What in the name of all that's horrible is that?' he asked Blob, with a gleam in his eye. 'It's a nightmare in my very own garden!'

You see, scary things were meat and drink to Pete. (Which doesn't mean he ATE them. More like he LOVED them.)

But anyway, Blob didn't answer. Because bassets can't talk. As you very well know.

But you know what they CAN do? When they're really, really scared? (Or when they're really, really scary, like the ones outside.)

'Aw-roooooo!'

That's what they can do. So that's what Blob did. At the top of his lungs.

'Shush, Blob!' said Pete, stroking him. 'You'll wake Dad!'

But, **'Aw-roooooo!'** came the answering cry, from outside.

Only a hundred times louder. Because there were a hundred times as many out there. (Except it wasn't quite a hundred times louder to Pete, of course, because the hounds were outside, and he was in. If it'd been a hundred times louder inside the house, then not only would his long-suffering dad have been wide awake by now, but the whole building would been shaken to its very foundations.)

Pete fetched his super-dooper beam-blaster, opened the window wide, and shone it up and down the street.

And guess what he saw?

A hundred long, low very black dogs! All gazing up at him with their glittery green eyes and howling…

'Aw-rooooooo!'

'They look like bassets!' said Pete, shutting the window quick. And the curtain. 'Are they bassets, Blob?'

And Blob, right there next to him, gave a little apologetic yes-yap.

'But I always thought you were the only one in town!' said Pete. 'So where have all the others come from? Are they friends of yours, from Newtown or Aber or somewhere?'

And Blob gave a little no-growl.

'Relatives, then?'

Another very definite no-growl.

'Well, who are they, and what are they doing here? I mean, what do you think they want, and why do you think they chose our house to howl at?' asked Pete. And then he got it. 'They're bassets, and they want you to join them! Do you want to join them, Blob?'

Blob jumped back into bed, shut his eyes and growled.

'I'll take that as a no,' said Pete. He pulled open the curtain again. Two hundred eyes were still out there, still glittering. 'Hmmm,' he said, unable to hide the excitement in his voice. 'I think this calls for further investigation.'

Pete threw on his night-time explorer gear, and headed for the door.

'Are you coming?' he asked Blob.

A little no-growl.

'Too much of a bag of nerves, by any chance?'

A little yes-yap.

'What? Aren't you my big brave basset?' Pete reached down and stroked his ever-faithful pup.

Blob gave him a little look. Then gave a little …
yap.

'...who comes out in the night and helps me set the world to rights,' added Pete.

Another look from those big mournful eyes. Another little yap.

'...who keeps me on the straight and narrow when I'm out and about, making things safe for daytime folk.'

A third little yap of agreement.

'And you know Dad says I always have to have someone with me on my night-time wanderings ... someone sensible... Well, aren't you that very someone, my little basset *bach*? Haven't you always been?'

One more look. One more little yap, and a tapping on the mattress with a tail.

'Thought so!' said Pete. 'Well, come on, then, my old faithful! Let's sort this pack of yowlers out before they wake the whole town!'

But by the time they got outside, the night bassets had given up on trying to get Blob to come out and join them.

And by the time Pete and Blob had tracked them down (easy enough with all that infernal yowling, which they carried on doing, all the way into town), the long, low, black dogs had made their way back over the bridge.

'Uh oh!' cried Pete, when he saw what they were up to.

The contents of every single rubbish bin between the roundabout and the Market Hall – the ones outside the chip shop, the kebab shop, the pizza shop, the Post Office and all four pubs – had been tugged out onto the ground. And the hungry dogs were snuffling around in the gubbins, trying to find something good to eat.

'Are they really bassets?' he whispered to Blob. 'I thought bassets were supposed to be all friendly and sensible, all good and clean and tidy, like you?'

And Blob gave a quiet little yes-yap. They ARE really bassets.

Followed by a cross little no-growl. These ones

are NOT those nice things you so kindly said I am. Because there are all sorts of bassets you know.

(Bassetts Allsorts? Got it?)

'Yeah, but bassets don't come in all sorts of colours, now do they?' said Pete. 'I mean, there's brown and black and white ones, like you. And I once saw one that was brown and white, and didn't have any black. And when I looked up bassets on the internet I saw a black and white one that didn't have any brown. But I've never seen an all-black one – in fact, I don't believe there are any – not in the real world, anyway,' said Pete.

And then he twigged. 'They're not just any old common-or-garden bassets like you, are they, Blob?'

Blob gave a little growl. (Which either meant no they're not, or meant stop saying I'm just a common-or-garden basset, I thought you said I was special. Or possibly both.)

'No, they're Night Dogs!' Pete realised, at last. 'They're Hounds from Hell!'

And Blob gave a yap, then a growl, then slunk in behind his master.

'Wow!' said Pete. 'First there's vampires … then werewolves … then a little bwca-man … and now a hundred Hell Hounds! We don't half get all sorts of weird and wonderfuls here in sleepy old Llani, in the middle of the pitch-dark night! But what are we going to do, Blob? How are we going to get rid of them?'

And then the Hounds from Hell spotted them.

'Aw-rooooo!'

The longest, lowest, fangiest one came racing towards them, full pelt, followed by every single one of the other ninety-nine nasties.

Well there's a time for talking and a time for running, and this was definitely a time for running.

So Pete and Blob were off like a shot, well two shots actually, back down Long Bridge Street, over the river, up Westgate Street, and through the front

door of 14 Swansea Terrace, slamming it JUST IN
TIME!

'Aw-roooo!' howled the Hell Hounds,
in the garden and on the doorstep.

And the longest, lowest, fangiest one pushed his
head through the cat flap.

'Aw-roooo!'

And his breath smelled DISGUSTING!

'What was that noise?' called Pete's dad, stirring
from his slumbers.

'Only Blob, having a bad dream,' said Pete,
rushing upstairs to reassure him with a little white
lie. 'Go back to sleep, Dad. Everything's fine!'

'We've got to do something, Blob!' hissed Pete, once
he was back down in the kitchen. 'We can't just
have them wrecking the place!' And then he had an
idea.

Quiet as a mouse, so the Hell Hounds wouldn't hear him, Pete eased open the back door and snuck down to his dad's shed, where he rummaged around in the dark. (He didn't bring his torch in case they spotted the light.)

Then, when he'd managed to find what he needed, he returned to the kitchen.

'Right, Blob,' he said. 'You're longer and lower than any of them, even that big scary boss one. So what we're going to do is...' And he produced, from behind his back, a big tin of paint and a brush. 'We're going to paint you black! Then they'll think you're one of them, and because you'll be the biggest meanest one of all, you can take over as boss of the Hell Hounds – well, they were trying to get you to join them anyway – and lead them out of town. What do you think?'

And you can guess what Blob thought of that. Not a lot.

'There's way too many of them!' said Pete. 'They'll trash the town, pee on the plants, poo on the paths, and then, to cap it all, if they're still here in the morning they'll terrify everyone! I mean, think of the effect on all the poor little kiddies on their way to school if a hundred Hounds from Hell are roaming the streets! Oh, we've got to get rid of them, Blob – come on, you and me, we're the Night-time Defenders, remember! It's our job to save Llani from attack!'

Blob knew he had no choice. So he lay on the kitchen floor, good as gold, sticking his tiny legs in the air, while Pete sploshed the brush in and out of the pot and painted him black all over, from his flippy-flop ears to the white little tip on the end of his long thin tail.

'Hmmm,' said Pete, looking at the floor. 'Maybe we should have put some newspaper down first. Oh well, never mind...'

Then Blob padded out into the night, to meet the Hounds from Hell.

Down the street, over the bridge he went, dripping great black blobs all along the pavement.

And there they were, down by the river, terrorising the poor ducks.

'Aw-rooooooo!' went the Hell Hounds.

'Quackity quack!' went the ducks.

(And I know we saw Pete and Blob having a bit of fun scaring the living daylights [the living night-lights actually, come to think of it] out of the poor unfortunate quackers when they were werewolves, but this is different, right? I mean, this is out-and-out NASTY!)

Blob stuck his head through the railings of the bridge and scowled down at them.

'Aw-rooooo!' he howled, in his bestest, deepest, scariest hell-howl of a voice.

And it wasn't a howl of friendship. It was a howl of challenge!

'That's it, Blob,' hissed Pete, following him at a safe distance. 'You tell them!'

The Hounds from Hell looked up from their duck-scaring. A hundred pairs of grisly green eyes, glittering in the pitch-dark night.

And then they charged!

The longest, lowest one reached Blob first. But Blob the Bravest Basset stood his ground.

'I'm longer and lower and darker than you are, mate, so BACK OFF!' growled Blob, in doggy language.

And the King of the Hell Hounds slunk back.

'A new king! A new king!' aw-rooed the hundred Hell Hounds. Well, ninety-nine of them anyway. Because the old king had slunk away, defeated, never to be seen again, hopefully.

And Blob knew what to do. He didn't really want to – he'd much rather be tucked up in his doggy-basket, safe from harm – but he knew he had to, to save the town…

So off he strode, at the head of the pack. And the remaining bunch of bassets followed their new leader, King Blob, up Long Bridge Street to the old black and white Market Hall, down Short Bridge Street to the river, up Penygreen Road (past the posh people, snoring away) and on out of town.

Blob led them on, plodding proudly at their head now (because it's quite nice being a royal, really, for a day or two), along the banks of the Clywedog, and all the way to the Hafren Forest.

Then through the trees and out of the trees they went, all in a great long line, till they came to the mouth of the River Severn, where they stopped for a paddle and a drink. Slurp, slurp.

Because it's thirsty work being a Hell Hound, what with all that howling and stuff.

Then all the way upwards, by the light of the harvest moon, till they came, with poor tired feet, to the very top of Plynlimon, the mighty mountain …

where the cloud was so thick that the ninety-nine Hell Hounds didn't notice brave Blob slink away out of sight … down the mountain, through the forest, along the riverbank, past the posh people, over the river (twice), and back to his lovely basket, in his lovely house, where his lovely Pete was tucked up in bed, with his fingers crossed.

(That's Pete with his fingers crossed, hoping his faithful companion would return safely, not Blob. Blobs don't have fingers. And if they did, they couldn't cross them, right?)

For though Blob had come to enjoy being a king for a few hours, with ninety-nine followers following, he didn't actually much fancy the life of a Hell Hound. Not without Pete, anyway.

But where did that leave the rest of the pack? Up the creek without a paddle, basically. (Not that Blob's a paddle, of course   he's a basset. And not that Plynlimon's a creek, but you get my drift…)

Because they didn't have a boss any more, the ninety-nine Hell Hounds. So there was no one to lead them back down off the bleak and windswept mountain, even when the cloud cleared and the sun rose over the wind farms to the east.

No one to take them back to Llani…

No one to lead them home to whatever hell-hole they'd crawled out of in the first place…

No, they didn't know where to go, and they didn't know what to do, and they didn't know how to make any sort of a decision because things had always been decided for them…

So there was nothing for it but to stay where they were, on the top of the mighty mountain, for the next day and the next, in fact from that day until this.

So here's a warning, my friend. If you ever manage to find yourself up on the top of Plynlimon, in the middle of the night, in the middle of a cloud (you'd be a right banana if you do, but then maybe you are, for all I know … I mean, you're reading this, aren't you?) and you hear a horrible, horrible sound…

'Aw-roooooo!'

Well, you'll know who it is. And you'll know who it ISN'T.

It isn't Blob the basset, because he's safely tucked up in his doggy basket in the kitchen of a house on Swansea Terrace. Or out on the prowl with his best mate Pete, protecting the good folk of Llani.

And it IS the Hounds from Hell. The Horrible Hounds from Hell. The Horrible HUNGRY Hounds from Hell!

Who haven't had a decent meal in I don't know how long.

So if I were you (and I'm glad I'm not), then I think you'd better…

RUN!

'RINGITY RING, RINGITY RING!'

It was seven o'clock in the morning, and Pete's dad's old alarm was ringing its bells off. (The one the little bwca-man had mended for him. Dad had grown to rather like it really, which is why it was still by his bed.)

Then, a few minutes later...

'Pete!' he roared, from the bottom of the stairs. 'What in the name of all that's extremely odd has been going on down here? The floor's all BLACK!' Silence. Then, 'Oh my stars – so is Blob!'

'Sorry about that, Dad,' said Pete, coming out onto the landing. 'We had a little bit of a night-time problem, but there's nothing to worry about. It's all sorted now, isn't it, Blob?'

Waggity wag. Yap yap.

Fancy Dress Night

'I LOVE Fancy Dress Night!' said Pete. 'Best night of the year, isn't it, Blob?'

Yappity yap. Wag wag.

'What are you dressing up as, Dad?' Pete called through to the other bedroom.

But he knew his dad wouldn't tell him. Nobody ever did.

Because the best bit about Fancy Dress Night was not knowing, and then meeting people on the street (or in the kitchen, in Pete and his dad's case) and trying to work out who it really was, and what they were supposed to be. And it might be people you

knew really well, but their disguise was so good that you wouldn't be able to tell who it was in a month of wet Wednesdays (and you get a few of THEM in mid-Wales).

'RINGITY RING!'

'Six o'clock!' yelled Dad. 'Time to go, guys!'

They met up down in the kitchen, and Pete was a bleeding zombie!

'*Ach a fi*, Pete! That's well-scary!' cried Dad. 'Have you been borrowing my make-up, by any chance?'

But his dad was a space-hopping astronaut!

'Out of this world, Dad!' Pete laughed. Then, 'Hey, is that my goldfish bowl on your head?'

(Don't even THINK of trying this at home, by the way. It is NOT a good idea!)

And Blob? Well, Blob was a Hound from Hell. He'd enjoyed himself so much the last time, he just had to give it another go.

(Pete's bedroom was a total write-off after painting his best dog black, of course, but never mind – they'd sort it in the morning.)

So off they all trooped into town.

And they did what they always did on Fancy Dress Night, which was head up to the Fish Shop, buy themselves each a big bag of steaming hot yumminess, then plomp down on a bench in the Market Hall and watch the town turn itself inside out.

Because every year, at six o'clock, what happens is that the police put up roadblocks to stop the cars coming in, and the whole of Llani changes completely, into a place just for people.

And just about every single resident comes out onto the streets, dressed up in the weirdest and most wonderful outfits you could imagine.

It's the most fun night of the year, in the friendliest town in Wales.

And it's like, for just those few magical hours, everybody becomes a Pete or a Blob. Yes, the whole town's chock-full of night-time adventurers.

And people pour in from all the towns and villages around, too, so there's literally thousands of them, all jam-packed up and down the short-but-wide streets, in the most outlandish costumes known to man, woman or bassct.

Pete's dad went off for a wander, when...

'Hey, there's another zombie, just like me!' cried Pete. 'I wonder who it is.'

And he jumped up from his bench and went over to have a look.

'Wow!' he said when he got up close and saw the empty eyes and broken teeth. 'That's really good – if I didn't know better, I'd think you really WERE a zombie!'

The zombie opened his mouth wide and grinned. And Pete, seeing the blood trickle out (and more of it drip from a gaping scar where the poor unfortunate's neck had been sliced wide open), knew he was in the presence of the REAL THING!

'Wow!' he said. 'I've always wanted to meet a real-live zombie – haven't you, Blob?'

But Blob was nowhere to be seen. Quite clearly he hadn't. (Though actually it's zombies who are supposed to be scared of dogs, not the other way round, as I think I told you before.)

'Oh, I'm not a real-LIVE zombie…' sighed the zombie. 'I'm a real DEAD one! Well, a real UNDEAD one, to be exact.'

'Coo-ul!' Pete rustled his bag, and held it under the zombie's nose. Well, where his nose would have been if he'd had more than just a hole, oozing snot. 'Fancy a chip?'

Blob barked, from under the bench. He was keeping well out of the way of zombies. Well, real ones, anyway. (And he wasn't barking because Pete was giving away the last of his chips. Blob had scoffed a load of them already.)

'What's the matter, boy?' said Pete, coming over to see him. 'You're not going back to being a scaredy-basset again, are you? Come on – Fancy Dress Night's a time for being brave!'

And then Pete heard the noise himself – a fiendish howl from down the bottom of Short Bridge Street.

'Aw-roooooo!'

And there it was, bounding towards them! Another Hell Hound!

'Hey, how did anyone else know to paint their dog black?' said Pete. 'It was only you and me that ever saw them, Blob!'

But, 'Oh my giddy aunt!' he gasped, as the Hell Hound came closer and Pete could tell, for certain sure – by its long, low fanginess and by the grisly-green glint in its eyes – that it wasn't just any old Llani dog in disguise.

'They must have found their way back down off the mountain, Blob!' he gasped.

But they hadn't. Because there was only one of them, not ninety-nine.

And it was giving Blob the dirtiest look in the whole history of dirty looks.

'Gulp!' gulped Blob, scuttling back under the bench.

Because you know who it was, don't you? Yes, it was the leader of the Hell Hounds! The one who'd been king before Blob had taken away his crown. The one who'd slunk away, never to be seen again, when Pete's best and bravest pet had stood up to him.

Only now he was back – back to get revenge! And Blob hadn't a hope in heck of hiding, unless…

'It's OK, Blob,' whispered Pete. 'I'll talk to him.'

And he went forward, holding up his bloodied hand.

'STOP!' he shouted. And the Hell Hound stopped.

'What do you want?' asked Pete. And the Hell Hound looked past him, at the cowering Blob.

'Oh, you want him, do you?' said Pete. 'You're not still angry with my best basset, just because he took your crown away, are you?'

And the Hell Hound snarled.

'Well, we don't want any dog fights here, not on Fancy Dress Night,' said Pete. 'There's lots of little kids about, and you'd scare them – a whole heap more than they want to be scared.

'So I'll tell you what we're going to do,' he went on, sternly. 'There's a competition for the best-dressed dog and I bet you'll win it, Mister Hell Hound, cos you look way more scary than Blob here, and he's the only other pet in fancy dress this year, as far as I can see.'

The Hell Hound frowned.

'I'll make sure you get a crown...' said Pete. 'So you'll be the King of the Hell Hounds again. Because Blob here doesn't want to be king any more, isn't that right?'

And Blob, from under the bench, quietly yapped.

'OK, stay here, the both of you,' said Pete. 'I'll be back now in a minute or two. But no squabbling! And no scaring the wits out of any children, or you'll cop it from me!'

And he gave the long, low, slavering hound the last of his chips, to keep him quiet – the poor dab looked like he hadn't had a good meal in a long time.

So Pete rushed home, made a placard saying 'HELL HOUND', ran back and hung it round the Night Dog's neck. Oh, and while he was at home he pulled an old Christmas Cracker crown, that he'd kept for some unknown reason, out of his bottom drawer.

And the infernal basset went up to the top of Great Oak Street to wait for the judging.

On the way through town Pete spotted another zombie. And another and another.

But they were all just pretend, like him – with loads of lipstick or ketchup or whatever it was slathered over their faces to look like blood.

And none of them were even half as scary-looking, never mind as eeky-beeky-yuksville as the real-live undead one Pete had met earlier.

There were about a hundred vampires too, wandering around the place, trying to look scary.

(So why is it that years ago everyone wanted to be Cinderella or Elvis or stuff, and now everyone wants to be vampires? That's what I want to know.)

'Don't worry, Dad,' said Pete, bumping into an astronaut. 'They're all just people in disguise.'

'Of course they're people in disguise,' said his dad, giving him a funny look. 'That's what fancy dress means.'

'Fair do's,' said Pete. 'But there ARE such things as real vampires! It's just these aren't them.'

'Yeah, maybe,' said his dad, not sounding convinced. 'But how can you actually tell?'

'Because real vampires, like Slurper Sue and Dracula's Daughter – you know, the ones we played football with way back when – never come out till after dark.'

'Don't they?' said Dad, scratching his head (well, his goldfish-bowl, actually). 'Did we? Wasn't that just a dream, Pete *bach*?'

Blob was still waiting under the bench. Pete told him about the people dressed up as vampires he'd just seen, and they had a good laugh about how silly it was.

'We might see some of our old friends later though, Blob, once it's dark,' said Pete, stroking his dog (and then wiping his hand on his jumper – it was all covered in black paint).

There was even a werewolf!

But Blob wasn't too worried about that one. He could tell by the fake fangs, and the dog collar around its neck, that it was just old Winston from number 27.

'The trouble is,' Pete whispered to Blob, 'there's just too many of them for me to keep under control. Everyone else thinks it's all just people in Fancy Dress, but some of them, like that zombie and the Hell Hound and heaven knows how many more, are the real deal – and they're going to cause no end of trouble – I can feel it in my bones. I've brought my whistle with me, to try and keep them all in line, but I don't know if it'll work – not if there's loads of them!

'Have no fear…' said a squeaky little voice. 'The bwca-man is here!'

'Hey, you're back!' cried Pete.

'What about my back? What's wrong with it?' The little fellow spun around, trying to look over his shoulder.

'No, I mean you've returned,' explained Pete, trying not to giggle.

'Of course I have,' came the reply. 'I wouldn't miss Fancy Dress Night – I've been coming for a hundred years or more.'

'Wow!' Pete was impressed. 'Anyway, it's good to see you again – give me five!'

'Five what?' said the minor miner. 'Five taps with my bangity-banger?'

'Hands up, then!' said Pete, instead. And he slapped the little fellow's spiky fingers.

'There's always loads of us bwcas here on Fancy Dress Night,' said the tiny man. 'Haven't you noticed before?'

'Well…' said Pete. 'I did used to wonder why quite so many kids were dressing up as miners… I never recognised any of them, so I always thought they must have been bussing them in from Aber or somewhere. And they'd never answer when I asked them who they were, so I thought maybe they only spoke Welsh.'

The bwca-man laughed. 'It's just nice to be able to wander round town for once without any of those horrid car-things belching smoke and noise all around the place, and trying to flatten us every time we try to cross the road. Can't abide them, me...' he said.

'Me neither,' said Pete. 'Town'd be much nicer without them.'

'Don't worry, we're never any trouble,' said the bwca. 'Not on Fancy Dress Night, anyway. No, the ones you have to look out for are all the ghosts and ghoulies, raising themselves up from the graveyard...'

'Really?' said Pete.

'Oh yes, and the witches and wizards, wandering around pretending they're humans...'

'Pretending they're witches and wizards…' added Pete, with a grin. 'And the zombies and Hell Hounds, too – I've seen them already.'

'Exactly,' said the little bwca-man. 'It's the one day of the year when all the creatures of the night are safe to come out before it's even dark, and parade up and down the streets, because everyone thinks they're just people in fancy dress. The thing is that some of them just can't stop themselves from scaring people – I mean, REALLY scaring people. So that's another good reason why me and my friends have to be here, to sort it all out.'

It was time for the judging of costumes. Everybody gathered in Great Oak Street, and the judges, including the much-loved local ex-Member of Parliament, Limpit Epoch, wandered up and down among them picking the best.

'Ta rum, ta ra!' came the announcement, over the tannoys. 'Can the following people please come up to the stage…!'

A rustle of excitement ran through the crowd.

'The Alien!' cried Limpit.

'The Dalek!'

'Dolly Pardon!'

'Lady GaGa…'

And they all went up and received their prizes.

Then, 'The Hell Hound!' he announced.

'Told you so,' whispered Pete, to the slavering creature standing just a little too close to Blob. 'You're king again!'

The Hell Hound made his way up onto the stage, and Limpit reached down and placed the crown for best-dressed pet (that Pete had passed him earlier) upon his head.

Then, 'The Zombie!' cried Limpit. 'The one with the revolting ear!'

'Wow! That must be me!' said Pete. And he followed the Hell Hound up, and had a medal hung round his neck.

'Hey, what about me?' came a voice, pushing his way through the crowd. 'I'm a better-looking zombie than him!'

It was the real zombie. And he was not a happy bunny.

Limpit Epoch took him to one side.

'We like to give the prizes to young people, if possible,' he whispered, trying to work out who it was he was talking to. 'Are you young, by any chance?'

'Young!' hissed the zombie. 'I'm not even alive!'

'Well then…' said Limpit, unfazed. He was used to people having tantrums, working in the House of Commons, like he did.

'Yes but I'm a REAL ZOMBIE!' growled the zombie. 'And if you don't give me a medal, I'll … I'll…'

He opened his mouth wide, and blood dripped out.

Limpit Epoch turned pale – even rival politicians didn't usually threaten to eat you – but suddenly a little miner-man hopped onto the stage, carrying a shiny silver star.

'This is for you,' the bwca hissed at the zombie. 'It's one I made earlier. Now get down off the stage and stop scaring people!'

'For me?' said the zombie. 'You made it specially for me?'

'That's what I said, didn't I?'

'Oh!' the zombie gasped. 'That's the nicest thing anyone's ever done for me! I've never had a silver star before!'

And he pinned it to his heart, causing foul-smelling pink goo to trickle out and down his chest.

Then off he went, into the night, grinning through his bloodied teeth, and singing a sweet little song.

'I'm a zombie,

I'm a zombie,

And I've got a horrible scar.

I'm a zombie,

I'm a zombie,

And I won a silver star...'

'And now,' cried Limpit Epoch, 'I would like to invite to the stage the one and only... Hillary Clinton!'

Only it wasn't Hillary Clinton. It was actually Mrs Walters, Pete's unfavourite neighbour. 'Congratulations, Mrs Clinton!' said Limpit. 'As one ground-breaking politician to another, it gives me great pleasure, on this wonderful occasion, in this historic place, to...'

'Jack it in, Epoch, and make with the prize, will you?' snarled the highly regarded American politician, grabbing the medal.

'BOOOOO!' cried Pete (dressed as a zombie, remember).

Then **'BOOOOO!'** cried the one hundred vampires, the seventy-two bwca-men, the alien, the dalek, the astronaut, Dolly Pardon, Lady GaGa – in fact everyone in the crowd...

Everyone except Blob and the Hell Hound, that is, who...

'Aw-rooooo-ed!' instead of boo-ed, at the top of their hound-dog voices.

Because not one of them was the slightest bit impressed at Mrs Walters' rudeness. It was NOT the sort of way you're supposed to behave, especially on Fancy Dress Night – grabbing prizes before they were even offered…

Insulting your very own, very famous, ex-Member of Parliament, who went out of his way every year to be there…

Mind you, they wouldn't have dared boo Mrs Walters to her face normally, oh no, not a one of them.

But the advantage of everyone being in fancy dress is that Mrs W, up there on the stage glowering down at the angry crowd, couldn't recognise anyone. So even if they were her neighbours – and THEY were the ones booing loudest, of course, because it wasn't just Pete and Blob she was always being crabby with – well, there's not a single thing Mrs Whingey Walters could do about it.

Hah! So much for dressing up as one of the most powerful women in the western world!

Just then, while Pete's attention was on the stage, Michael Jackson ran past and pinched his medal, singing…

'I'm BAD … I'm BAD … you know it!'

'Hey,' yelled Pete. 'That's mine!'

And he took off after him, followed by Blob, the Hell Hound, the zombie and the little bwca-man.

They chased him down Short Bridge Street, over the river and caught him on the other side.

'You're MEAN as well as bad, whoever you are – stealing people's medals!' cried Pete, tearing off his mask.

And guess who it was? Billy Beggs, the playground bully!

Well, the Hell Hound pinned him to the ground, the little bwca-man tapped him on the knee-cap with his hammer, three times in quick succession… (Only gently, though. Pete made sure of it.)

And the zombie (the real one, that is) lay down next to Billy Beggs and breathed zombie-breath all over his face till he was begging for mercy. (It's like a mixture of garlic, manure and death, is zombie breath. Just so you know.)

'Stop! Stop! I'll never be nasty again!' sobbed Billy.

'You'd better not be, you big baby,' said Pete, 'or me and my friends here will come and find you while you're sleeping, and … well, I won't tell you what we'll do, but you're not going to like it. Not one little bit…'

And then, with a crash of drums, a screech of feedback, a screaming of guitars and a roaring of rock, the music started.

Live music, on Long Bridge Street.

More, pouring out of the Lentil Café, onto Great Oak Street.

Even more, and louder still, raising the roof in the United Services Club.

Dancing! Shouting! Fun, fun, fun!

And as if that wasn't enough, the vampires appeared. The REAL ones, now that it was dark enough for them to wander about at will.

Yes, Vladimir and Veronica, skipping down the street, arm-in-arm… Gnasher giving Dracula's Daughter a twirl… Slurper Sue, Eeky Edward and Revolting Ronnie eyeing up the butcher's window (like they might be considering a midnight raid) … Frankenstein's Folly and Horrible Harvey having a friendly little chat with Limpit Epoch.

And lastly, but definitely not leastly, Bloodsucking Bert – chasing Mrs Walters all the way home.

But where was Pete, while all this mayhem and madness was going on?

He was heading home – down Long Bridge Street, over the river, up Westgate, turn right into Swansea Terrace – with his faithful low-slung basset at his side.

'Let's leave them to it, Blob. I don't know about you but I'm just about done in, me. So if there's any more trouble,' he said, 'I'm sure the little bwca-men can sort it out. Fancy Dress Night is a barrel of laughs but, to tell you the truth, I'm starting to think I prefer quiet nights, myself – when it's just you and me, the darkness, and whatever the night may bring...'

And what did Blob say?
Waggity wag. Yap yap.